This edition published by Parragon Books Ltd in 2014

Parragon Books Ltd
Chartist House
15–17 Trim Street
Bath BA1 1HA, UK
www.parragon.com

Written by Barbara Jean Hicks
Illustrated by Olga T. Mosqueda

ISBN 978-1-4723-7748-7

Printed in China

From the movie

DISNEY

FROZEN

An Amazing Snowman

Written by Barbara Jean Hicks
illustrated by Olga T. Mosqueda

PaRragon

Bath·New York·Cologne·Melbourne·Delhi
Hong Kong·Shenzhen·Singapore·Amsterdam

Olaf is not
your everyday
snowman.

He
walks.

He
talks.

He even
sings.

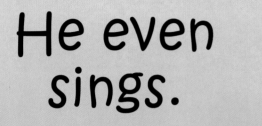

But those aren't the only things
that make him special!

Olaf is special
because

he sees the
best in
everyone.

His brother,
Marshmallow,
is a playful
fellow....

Sven the reindeer
is forever trying to
kiss his nose ...

and Queen Elsa and Princess Anna
always include him
in their games.

Olaf is special
because

he finds
beauty in
every day ...

and because he dreams.

Olaf dreams about sandcastles ...

and ships sailing to new horizons ...

Olaf dreams about soaring in the SKY ...

and picking fresh fruit …

Olaf is special because in his eyes, summer

or
winter,

every day is an
adventure ...

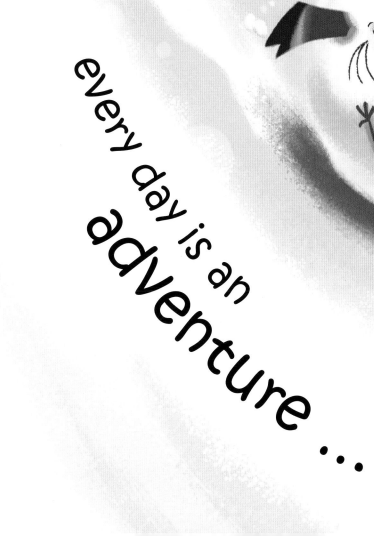

and
every
night
shines.

Olaf is
special because
he knows
that every
ending ...

is a chance for a new beginning ...

and
a
chance ...

for a
nice warm
hug!

The
End